Published by Curious Fox, an imprint of Capstone Global Library
Limited, 264 Banbury Road, Oxford, OX2 7DY – Registered
company number: 6695582

www.curious-fox.com

Squishy Taylor and the Vase that Wasn't
Text copyright © 2016 Ailsa Wild
Illustration copyright © 2016 Ben Wood
Series design copyright © 2016 Hardie Grant Egmont
First published in Australia by Hardie Grant Egmont 2016

Published in British English in 2018 by Curious Fox

ISBN 978 1 78202 771 3

21 20 19 18 17
10 9 8 7 6 5 4 3 2 1

A CIP catalogue for this book is available from the British Library.

Printed and bound in India

and the
Vase that Wasn't

Ailsa Wild
with art by BEN WOOD

Curious Fox
a capstone company-publishers for children

For Jimmie and Goldie – and your
ridiculous, brave, loving mama.
– Ailsa

For Tim, the best twin brother I have.
– Ben

Chapter One

I slip off my shoes at the door and swing them by the laces. The lobby of our apartment building is like an ice-skating rink if your shoes are off. I launch into a **giant skid** to the lift, finishing in a crouch like a surfer.

My bonus sister Vee takes off her shoes and slides after me. She stumbles over me when she catches up. Her twin, Jessie, walks in normally behind us. I call

them my bonus sisters because they were a bonus when I moved in with my dad and their mum, Alice.

Mostly they're an awesome bonus. Like now. Vee is lying on the floor laughing. When I try to pull her up, she just **slides along** on her back. It makes me laugh until I'm gasping.

When she finally stands up, the lift doors slide open.

There's a man inside, shouting into his phone. "It's gone! It's gone!" he says as he steps out of the lift. "I've been robbed. . . . Yeah, exactly, or **haunted!**"

His eyes are big, and he's got a crazy look on his face. "It just . . . disappeared!" he says.

"What just disappeared?" Jessie asks, sounding like a grown-up. She steps up beside us with her rucksack neatly on her back.

Jessie's the oldest of the twins, but only by forty-seven minutes. Vee is staring at the man, and I'm trying not to laugh.

"My vase is gone!" the man says into his phone. "My great-grandmother's Ming Dynasty vase."

"Stolen?" I ask, remembering the adventure we had when we thought our next-door neighbour was robbed.

"No, *disappeared*," the man says to me, waving his phone. "My doors were locked. Nothing else had moved. It was like a ghost had been there."

He sounds weirdly excited. Then he seems to realize that he's been talking about ghosts to three kids. He puts his phone back to his ear.

"Sorry, I got distracted," he says into his phone. "Yes. The police! I should go to the police." He stumbles through the lobby doors and out onto the pavement.

Jessie swipes her key card and presses the lift button. We watch the man stand outside and wave his arms around.

I **giggle** and want to keep watching, but Jessie pulls us into the lift.

"I don't know why he didn't just call the police," Jessie says.

This is so weird. The cool kind of weird. I do the man's crazy grin and flapping hands and say, **"Haunted!"**

It comes out sounding half like the man and half like Scooby Doo.

We laugh, collapsing against the lift wall.

"You're hilarious, Squishy," Jessie says.

That's right. **My name is Squishy.**

Squishy Taylor. It's a special nickname my parents gave me when I was little.

I love that Jessie said I was hilarious. Sometimes she just rolls her eyes when I think I'm funny and she doesn't. Not this time. It makes my laugh even bigger.

We're still laughing when the lift opens at our floor.

Mr Hinkenbushel is there, waiting for the lift. He's our next-door neighbour. He's also the **grumpiest man in the universe** and an **undercover**

policeman. He frowns at us. We freeze because one of the rules Dad and Alice have is that we have to be quiet and not disturb him.

"Hurry up and get out of the lift. What are you waiting for? Rotten kids."

We stumble out past him. I bump him with my rucksack, and he growls.

Seriously. **He growls.**

And this isn't even the worst part. When he shouts, **he spits.**

When the lift closes, we all breathe out. Then we run down the hall to our apartment.

Jessie pushes open the door. Alice says, "Hi, kids," from where she's typing at the kitchen table. She is working at home because it's Tuesday.

The twins say, "Hi, Mum."

I say, "Hi, Alice."

Alice and my dad moved in together when they had Baby. I used to live with my mum, but she got a job in Geneva, Switzerland. I decided to stay with Dad.

Baby is sitting in the middle of the rug. Jessie's old collection of Barbies is spread out around him. He picks up one without a head and waves her around excitedly. She flies out of his hand, but it takes him a moment to realize she's gone.

We all laugh at his surprised face and **swoop down on him.**

"Baby-Baby-Baby," Vee says in a **gooey growl**, sprawling onto her stomach beside him and mushing her nose into his big cheek.

I drop my rucksack and do a fast spin-roll over the sofa. I stop right in front of his feet. I jiggle his legs. "You little fluffy-fluff-fluff," I say.

Jessie has nuzzled in from the other side, and Baby squeals and giggles and flaps his arms around.

"Mum, can we have toast out on the balcony today?" Jessie asks, winking at us.

Jessie always knows how to ask for special treats. And it's a real treat to be on the balcony, because the door is in Alice and Dad's room. We're allowed to go anywhere else in our apartment, but their bedroom is off limits. We have to have **extra-special permission** to go out on the balcony.

"Yep, OK. Fine," Alice says. "Just don't talk to me for another fifteen minutes." Her nose is about two centimetres from her computer screen, and she hasn't stopped typing for one second.

"**Yay!**" Vee says, kicking my rucksack out of the way and heading for the toaster.

"Hey, Alice," I say, sliding some more Barbies to Baby with my foot. "You should have seen this crazy guy in the lobby–"

"Squishy, I said don't talk to me."

Even my **bonus mum** calls me Squishy. My real name is Sita. I'm named after my grandma, but people only call me that when I'm in serious trouble.

Vee hasn't given up on our story. "But the guy in the lobby said–"

"Do you want to have your toast on the balcony or not?" Alice asks, actually looking up from her screen.

"Balcony!" we say in unison. I get out the big jar of peanut butter. When I need to be, **I'm silent as a ninja.**

When we work as a team, the three of us are *fast*.

As soon as we're on the balcony, we see Haunted Guy hurrying back up the street with Mr Hinkenbushel beside him.

"I guess **Haunted Guy** found the police station," I say with my mouth full of peanut butter on toast.

I lean my elbows on the balcony and look down. My curls get stuck in my mouth with my next bite of toast. I try to **spit my hair out**, and the chewed toast goes too. It tumbles down past all the other balconies. We all laugh, and a few more pieces fall out. Luckily, they don't hit Mr Hinkenbushel.

A few minutes later, we hear Haunted Guy's voice. He's on the balcony right above us.

Chapter Two

"Yes, *all* the locks!" Haunted Guy says. "*Everything* was locked!" He sounds kind of upset but mostly like I would feel – like he's having an adventure.

We hear Mr Hinkenbushel's familiar grumpy voice.

"Absurd . . . security cameras . . . ridiculous to say it just disappeared."

The talking drops to mutters so we can't hear words anymore.

Jessie whispers, "What are they saying?"

I don't know. I really want to hear. I put my finger to my lips and climb, as quietly as I can, onto the balcony table. Jessie gives me a look, but I don't care. I stretch my neck, trying to hear.

Haunted Guy's voice is quiet, but I catch a few words. "No, nothing else moved. Only the vase."

Then more murmurings.

I **feel the table wobble**, and realize Vee is climbing up beside me. She's pointing, showing me the long beams holding the balcony over our heads. If I stand on my **tippiest tiptoes**, I can get my hands halfway around a beam. It's not exactly like monkey bars, but it's close enough.

Jessie is shaking her head, her eyes wide. Vee offers me a step with both hands. I haul myself up with my biceps, like a chin-up, with Vee's hands helping.

From here, I can hear Haunted Guy better. He's saying, "I'll have to call my sister. It's from the **Ming Dynasty**. Absolutely priceless. Came from the **Opium Wars**. It simply disappeared. I was only gone for one night."

A door clicks. They've gone inside. Ming Dynasty. Opium Wars. What does it all mean? I look down at Jessie, then past Jessie to the street. It's eleven storeys down. **That's a long way down.**

I suddenly realize how close I am to the edge of the balcony. Now that I'm standing on the table, the railing is too low to stop me from falling over the edge. My hands are slippery and shaky. I can't hold on. I **drop, stumble and crash** my way back to the floor as quickly as I can. I take a couple of minutes to let my heart stop beating so hard.

Then I tell Jessie and Vee everything I heard Mr Hinkenbushel and Haunted Guy saying.

We stare at each other.

A priceless vase just disappeared from an apartment when all the doors were locked tight.

"Isn't that cool?" I ask.

"That's freaky!" says Vee.

"We have to Google this," says Jessie.

Then Baby starts crying inside.

Alice calls, "Homework! Now!"

We run into the living room, and I do a leapfrog over Vee onto the sofa. She falls on top of me, giggling.

"Oops! Ow – get off me!" I say, laughing.

Baby stops crying and does his **cutest chuckles**.

Jessie sets up her homework at the kitchen table and starts working with her head down. Vee and I spread our things out. Then we make up a game where you pretend to jump on Baby and miss just at the last minute. He thinks it's the best thing ever.

Alice starts making dinner in the kitchen. Then Dad walks in wearing his cycling clothes. His legs look so skinny and funny.

"Hello!" He comes around and gives me the **traditional forehead-kiss**.

"Hi, Tom," say Jessie and Vee. Then Dad gives them forehead kisses too.

I'm not used to them getting the same treatment as me. I need more from him. **I jump onto his back** while he's cuddling Alice.

"Ooof!" Dad says. We all stumble into the counter, and Alice giggles.

"You're getting **a bit too heavy** for that, Squisho," Dad says.

I slide down his back onto the floor. "Hey, did you know a vase disappeared from the apartment upstairs?"

Dad grins. "Really?" he says. "And I suppose Mr Hinkenbushel stole it, right?"

Dad's joking with me, because every time something goes wrong, I think it's Mr Hinkenbushel's fault.

"DAD," I say, grabbing onto his legs. "It wasn't Mr Hinkenbushel. It was a burglar. Or a ghost!"

"OW!" he says. "You're scarier than a burglar and a ghost combined."

I grab his legs again. He drags me a little way down the hall for fun. I let go so he can take a shower.

But then I start to wonder about the missing vase. Mr Hinkenbushel is going to be investigating. What will he find?

Chapter Three

After dinner, I sit on the sofa and call Mum on Skype in Geneva.

"Hi, Squishy. Hi, Jessie," Mum says, waving from her desk.

I didn't realize Jessie was standing behind me.

"Hi, Devika," Jessie says, leaning her elbows on the back of the sofa.

"What's going on?" Mum asks.

"Well," Jessie says. "We know it's Squishy's special iPad time, but we desperately need to Google things while she's talking to you."

Vee leans over my other shoulder. "So we're here to hurry you up."

Mum laughs, but I feel a little bit annoyed. First they both get my special

Dad—forehead—kiss, then they crowd in on my special Skype time with Mum.

"What information do you need to Google?" Mum asks.

Jessie barely lets Mum finish asking. "We're wondering about Ming Dynasty vases and the Opium Wars."

How does she remember that stuff? She wasn't even the person who heard it first.

"Well," says Mum, leaning back. "I can tell you about the Opium Wars." Of course she can. Mum knows everything about international relations. That's why she works at the United Nations. "Basically, the Chinese refused to buy opium from the British, so the British went to war with the Chinese."

"What?" Vee says. "Why?"

"To force the Chinese to buy opium," Mum says.

"But that's crazy!" Vee says.

Mum does her sideways smile and nods. "Yes, pretty crazy," she agrees.

"So then," Jessie says, scooting around to sit next to me, "what would it mean that a vase was 'acquired during the Opium Wars'?"

Mum laughs. "It means that a British pirate probably stole the vase from its rightful owner."

"Pirates!" Vee says. "Awesome!" She makes a hook hand and wrinkles her face and says, "Arrrrgh!"

Mum laughs even harder. She actually thinks Vee is funny.

"OK, guys," I say. "Go away! Let me talk to my mum now."

"Sorry, sweetie," Mum says. "Gotta run. My next meeting started three minutes ago. Love you, Squishy."

"Love you," I say, even though I'm not ready for her to go.

"Bye, kids!" She waves.

"Bye, Devika!" the twins say, and then Jessie pushes the hang-up button.

"Awesome," Jessie says and takes the iPad away.

It makes me grumpy. She starts reading all kinds of boring things about the Opium Wars and the British in China. I am the total opposite of caring. I just wanted to talk to my mum.

On the bus to school, my bonus sisters and I **squash together** on one seat. The two ladies opposite us are looking at one phone. They're watching a funny YouTube video that's been going around. It's of a kid dancing. I recognize the music. Vee smirks at me.

When it finishes, one of the ladies points at the phone. "Did you see this?"

Her friend takes it from her and reads aloud. *"City apartment haunted by the vengeful ghost of ancient Chinese soldier. Priceless Ming Dynasty vase 'stolen by spirits,' says owner."* They look at each other and both burst out laughing.

"Can I see?" I ask, leaning over and trying to see their phone.

"Of course," one of the ladies says.

"Squishy!" Jessie says, elbowing me. I elbow her back and point to the picture on the lady's phone. It's a tall, white vase that's been painted blue with beautiful blue trees and mountains.

The bus stops outside our school, and we pile off together, saying, "Thanks, bye!" to the ladies.

We start to cross the road, and Vee asks, "Do you think there's really a ghost in our apartment building?"

Her face looks pale and worried.

Then I remember. Vee and her friends had a sleepover party a few weeks ago. They **watched a horror film** they weren't supposed to watch. It scared Vee so much that Alice had to go and pick her up in the middle of the night.

Now she has the same look on her face that she had when she came home from the sleepover.

She grabs my sleeve. "Maybe a ghost *did* take the vase."

Vee looks really, really scared. I feel bad for her. But I know the best thing to do with fear. **Face it head—on**.

"Let's sneak out tonight and try to find the ghost," I say, pushing open the door to our school. It gives me a kind of excited, creepy feeling, but Vee turns even whiter. Part of me knows we won't see anything, but I think it would be fun anyway.

Jessie has an even better idea. She always has better ideas. "Let's hack into the apartment's security footage from that night and see what *really* went on."

Genius.

That's our Jessie. She's **so boring** one minute and **so brilliant** the next.

Chapter Four

Jessie and Vee don't usually talk to me at school because they're five and a half months older than me. Which is fine – I like my school friends better than theirs. My friends and I spend lunch and breaktime playing monkey bar tag. If you touch the ground, you're it. I'm **super-ninja** at it since I started rock climbing and doing bunk-bed acrobatics. I'm like a monkey goddess with a hundred arms.

Vee passes just as I'm doing a **kick up** to the top bar. She's talking to her friends from the horror film sleepover.

"Really," she says. "An actual ghost."

"Ooooh," one of them says, sounding impressed. **"Aren't you terrified?"**

Then I get tagged on the shoulder.

After dinner, I tell the grown-ups that I'm going to call Mum on Skype. I grab the iPad and go to our bedroom. Jessie and Vee follow me, and we all sit on Jessie's bed.

I type: **Love you, Mum. Way too much homework, talk tomorrow night?**

She sends a **row of kisses**, which is short for: I love you, I'm busy too.

Done.

I hand the iPad to Jessie so she can **work her hacker magic**. Another message pops up on the screen. Mum has been thinking.

Wait. Since when do you WANT to do your homework?

We all laugh.

Jessie sends Mum a cute wink emoji. Then she gets down to work. It's no fun watching Jessie Google things. She flicks between windows so fast, you can't actually read anything.

"Ah. Right," Jessie mutters. "How do I get into this security footage?" Jessie stops at a screen with some instructions and a password box. "Hmm. It says that all residents have password access to security footage from their own floor for two weeks. After that–"

"Boring!" I say.

Which gives me an idea.

"What do you think Not-Boring Lady's doing?" I ask Vee.

We do **desk-leap-scrambles** up to Vee's bunk, and then we do some **rolling-spin-drops** down to mine. We take turns looking at Not-Boring Lady through the telescope.

Her light is still on. Not-Boring Lady is known to some people as the Chief of Special Secret Undercover Operations. Our bedroom window looks across the street into her quiet work room, so all we ever see her do is type. But now we know all about her secret not-boring job.

We wave to her, but she doesn't look up from her typing.

Our telescope is really good. It's built for looking at the stars. Right now, we're looking at every single one of Not-Boring Lady's eyelashes.

We jump up and down and wave our arms crazily in front of the window, but she doesn't notice us.

"I wonder what she's working on?" I ask while Vee looks.

"AHA!" Jessie says from her bunk. "The easiest password ever! I'm in."

We drop onto her bunk. The screen is divided into two black-and-white scenes showing the twelfth floor hall. It's like two grainy YouTube videos next to each other. One shot is from the lift, and the other is from the stairwell door. They're both empty.

"The thief must have come in through the balcony," I say.

"I haven't searched the right time yet," Jessie says, sliding the fast-forward bar down the bottom. "Let's look at when Haunted Guy first found out. It was when we got home from school, right?"

Jessie slides the bar to that time, and suddenly there's Haunted Guy coming out through his door, waving his arms, and running towards the lift. She slides some more. We see Haunted Guy and Mr Hinkenbushel walking back together.

"OK, sooo–" Jessie says, sliding the bar even more to the time the vase might have disappeared.

"There!" Vee and I say at the same time. Jessie freezes the screen.

We all stare at it. For the first time, I really, truly believe in ghosts.

It's an ancient Chinese soldier, standing perfectly still. He's wearing fancy armour

carved with **dragons** and has a helmet covering his eyes. He's holding a spear. He doesn't move once.

Jessie slides the time bar forwards and backwards. At 11.59, there's nothing. Then at midnight, the ghost suddenly appears. It stands absolutely still for exactly thirteen seconds. You might not think thirteen seconds is a long time, but when you're **looking at a ghost**, I promise you, it is. After thirteen seconds, the soldier ghost fades away and disappears.

"No way!" Jessie whispers. "No way, no way, no way!"

Vee's hand is gripping mine. Hard.

Jessie keeps sliding the time bar back and forth, like she'll find something we've missed.

Then the screen freezes.

A text box flashes up on the screen, and the words **Don't you dare** appear in it, one letter at a time. It's like there's a ghost inside the iPad. Vee gives a little scream.

Then a profile picture loads beside the words. It's Mr Hinkenbushel.

Mr Hinkenbushel is actually writing to us on our screen: **You nosy kids**, he says. **If you do this again, I'll take your iPad for evidence. Go outside and play hopscotch.** The security screen slides away, and we're back to the Google homepage.

Jessie gasps and says, "How did he do that?"

"It was a ghost. A ghost." Vee says.

Jessie says, "It was Mr Hinkenbushel. He must be watching the security system as part of his investigation."

"But before that," Vee says. "There was a ghost before that."

I'll admit that I'm a little bit scared of the ghost. But I'm more worried about Mr Hinkenbushel. I don't want him to be in our iPad. I really don't want him to spy on us. The iPad is the only way for me to talk to Mum. It makes me kind of angry, thinking Mr Hinkenbushel could watch and listen when I'm talking to her.

"Can Mr Hinkenbushel see what we're doing on the iPad whenever he wants?" I ask.

Jessie frowns. "Eww. No. Why would

you think that, Squishy?"

"Because he was **just right there**, talking to us."

"I think," Jessie explains, "he can only talk to us from the security website. Maybe because he's investigating, he can see what anyone on that website is doing." She pauses and shakes her head. "He can't just look at us anytime. That would be illegal."

"Oh." I feel a big wash of **relief**.

Vee looks half-scared, half-angry. "I can't believe *that's* what you're talking about," she hisses. "Don't you even care that **we saw a ghost**?"

Chapter Five

Alice sends us off to bed, and we go quietly. The image of that ghost keeps appearing and disappearing in my mind like it did on the footage.

Vee whispers to us in the dark, "If a ghost can steal a vase, what else could it do?"

"It can't really be a ghost," Jessie says. "It's got to be **some kind of hoax.**"

"It could be either," I say. Whatever it is, it's a mystery, so I'm happy.

In the night, I wake up because Vee is climbing out of bed. It scares me, and I lie there, clutching my blanket. A few minutes later, Alice brings Vee back and tucks her in.

"Don't be scared," Alice whispers. "I'm here." She stands next to Vee's pillow and murmurs for a while. My heart slows back down to normal, and I fall asleep before Alice leaves.

Jessie looks extra thoughtful over breakfast, but she doesn't say much. Vee is stirring her porridge without putting any in her mouth. Baby **smashes** his apple against the table, throws the tiny pieces all over the floor and laughs. He's not scared of anything.

We don't talk about the vase at all, but the whole day I'm a little bit tingly all over because I know that something big is happening.

"Hey, you three," Dad says to me, Jessie and Vee when we get home from school. "Someone got an email from Geneva today."

"**Woohooo!**" I shout and run to him. Emails from Mum usually mean film vouchers or music credit.

He shakes his finger, grinning. "Not for you, Squisho. It's for somebody else."

He passes the iPad over to Jessie.

I just stare. *Mum* emailed *Jessie*? The world feels wrong. I can feel my eyes prickling hot, and I don't know what to do. Dad gives all of us exactly equal **forehead-kisses**. That used to be my special Dad-hello. And suddenly, I feel hot-hot, really-really angry.

That's **my** dad and **my** mum. It's fine that they live apart from each other. I got used to that a long time ago. It's fine that I have to share a bedroom with my bonus sisters. They actually are an awesome bonus. But I need *some* special things – some things that are only for me.

I whack the butter knife down on the counter, nearly break the peanut butter jar and slam the cupboard door closed. No one notices.

Dad asks Vee how school was, looking concerned because she's so quiet. Jessie sits at the table, reading an email from *my* mum.

No one notices me **banging** plates.

"Wow!" says Jessie. She keeps reading silently. Then she says, "Oh, *what*?"

There's another pause. What does she think we're going to do? Beg to be told what she's reading?

"No way!" Jessie says.

I actually hate her.

"What is it? What does it say?" Vee asks, falling for Jessie's game.

"So . . ." Jessie says, sounding all important. "Devika sent me an article about the Opium Wars. It says there were forty-seven matching vases in a temple, and a British admiral killed all the priests and stole all the vases."

"**Whoa**," Vee says, pulling her chair closer. "He killed all the priests?"

Jessie nods and says, "Later, he sold the vases for lots of money all around the world."

I'm listening, even though I wish I wasn't. Even though I wish Mum had sent the email to me, not Jessie. I can't help feeling a bit interested.

"Now there's an international treaty," says Jessie, "between a lot of museums, to give the vases back. But they haven't found them all. They think some greedy people are keeping them a secret."

Dad grins. "This is totally Devika's kind of thing. She loves getting involved in righting old wrongs."

He's right about that. Mum calls it **"justice work"**. It's what she loves about her job.

Then Jessie squeals, which wakes up Baby, who starts **howling**.

"What?" Dad and I ask.

"It's the same vase!" Jessie says. "The one upstairs is one of the forty-seven!"

I run to look over her shoulder. Dad and Vee crowd in. Jessie shows us the picture from Mum's article. It's the exact same photo as the one we saw on the lady's phone on the bus.

Jessie does a search for the news article then flicks between the two pictures.

"So. The vase upstairs was stolen from a temple by a very **greedy** British admiral," I say.

Vee looks grim. "And then stolen back by a ghost," she says.

"What ghost?" Dad asks.

Just then, there's a knock on the door. I run to answer it, because I'm closest.

It's Mr Hinkenbushel.

"I need to talk to you, Mr Taylor," he says, as if I'm not standing right in front of him. "Your kids have been **hacking** the building's security footage."

Chapter Six

Dad and Alice have taken Baby to Mr Hinkenbushel's apartment. It feels weird, because Mr Hinkenbushel yelled at Alice once, and they're not friends. But sometimes adults who don't like each other become **allies** to gang up on kids.

We're left sitting on the living room floor, waiting to find out what kind of trouble we're in. It's dinnertime, but no one's cooking.

Vee looks worried and scared. "It just had to be a ghost," she says. "There's just no way that was not a ghost." She's jiggling her knee nervously.

"It has to be a hoax," Jessie says. "So someone could steal that vase."

"How *could* it be a hoax?" Vee asks, her voice a little bit high.

"Maybe it was someone in a costume," Jessie suggests.

"But what about how it *faded away*?"

Jessie shrugs. Now Vee looks even more creeped out.

I'm creeped out too but in a good way. Is it a hoax or a haunting? Either way, it's awesome.

"Well," I say, "the main thing is that the vase needs to be returned to China."

The others nod.

Then I think of something else. "Why do you think Mr Hinkenbushel wanted to stop us from looking at the ghost?"

"It wasn't a ghost," Jessie says.

"How do you know?" Vee asks. It is getting darker outside, and she's looking more and more nervous. There's something kind of sad about the way she jumps and looks around whenever there's a noise.

"I don't know," Jessie says. "Let's take a look at the security footage again now, while Mr Hinkenbushel is distracted with Tom." She starts looking around for the iPad.

"Dad took the iPad," I say. I saw him slip it under his arm on his way out.

Jessie stands still. Even she doesn't know what do to next.

We need a plan. Vee is jiggling even more now and biting her lip.

"In the horror film, they did this thing to scare off the ghost," Vee says. "They chanted and drew a magic circle. One man held a big black book."

It sounds exciting. It sounds like a scary kind of fun. But Jessie's shaking her head. I can tell she's worried about how seriously Vee is taking the whole ghost thing.

"We need to look at that security footage again somehow," Jessie says. "Or get someone else to."

"What about Not-Boring Lady?" I say.

"What about her?" Jessie asks.

"Well, she *is* the Chief of Special Secret Undercover Operations," I say.

Vee looks hopeful. "Do you think we could signal her?"

I scramble up from the floor and grab the torch from under the sink. I switch it on. It's pointed at my eyes, so I blind myself. It's definitely bright enough.

We all run into our bedroom.

"Is she there?" Vee asks.

She's there.

I shine the torch at the window, but it just reflects back at our faces. Jessie takes the torch and pushes it against the glass. She scrapes it from side to side.

I do a **high-kick** up to my bunk, stare through the telescope and think, *Look at us, Not-Boring Lady*. But she just keeps typing. Her face is all **concentratey**.

Vee is getting more desperate. "This isn't working."

"OK, what about this?" Jessie runs to the wall and flicks our bedroom light **on-off-on-off-on-off-on**. Our whole window blinks. Not-Boring Lady has to notice that. She doesn't.

"Not-Boring Lady, help!" Vee shouts, even though we all know she can't hear us.

"We could email her," Jessie begins, then stops. "But we don't have the iPad."

It's starting to feel like Dad and Alice are never coming home, and Vee looks **pretty panicky**.

"OK, you know what we should do?" I say. "You know who *would* believe us?"

The others look at me.

"Haunted Guy!" I say. "Maybe he'd let us look at the ghost on *his* computer."

We stare at each other for a moment.

Vee says, "You're right. If anyone is going to believe us, he will."

"Should we visit him?" I ask. "Now?"

That's when Dad and Alice walk in with Baby. And they are angry.

We eat cheese toasties for dinner in silence. Alice puts Baby to bed, and Dad Skypes Mum. He talks to her for a long time – probably all about how naughty

I am. When he comes back with Mum still on the iPad, it should be my turn to talk to her.

But it's not. Dad props up the iPad on the kitchen table and makes us sit where we can all see Mum.

"Family meeting," he says as Alice steps in quietly, closing Baby's door.

I groan. "Family meeting" translates to "Adults talk too much. Kids get bored." I just want to visit Haunted Guy.

They tell us to use the internet responsibly and to be safe online. It's **exactly as interesting** as I guessed it would be.

"From now on, we're going to have a new rule," Alice says. "You girls are only allowed to use the iPad in the living room."

Jessie protests.

I look at Mum, who has on a serious face. "But what about when I Skype with you?" I ask.

She shakes her head. "Sorry, Squisho. Living room only. All of you just lost your privileges."

We do **pleading faces**. We promise to be **so, so, so good**. The grown-ups don't budge.

Then we have to hang up before I get a chance to really talk to my mum. Again. That's the third night in a row that we haven't really talked.

And it's too late to visit Haunted Guy. They make us go straight to bed. We're not even tired.

Vee actually **climbs the ladder** to her bunk. I don't think I've ever seen her do that. Alice turns off the light, and I hear Vee's breathing get low and fast.

I don't care. At least her mum kisses her goodnight. I'm not even allowed to talk to my mum.

Chapter Seven

I wake up in the dark with something touching my face.

"Can you hear that?" Vee whispers. She's hanging over the side of the bunk. Her fingers are tapping my ear.

I sit up fast and swat at her hands. **"No! Wait! What?"** I say.

I listen for a while, but I don't hear anything at all.

"We need to do that thing they did in the film to get rid of the ghost," Vee says, sounding scared.

"Vee, go back to sleep."

In the morning, Vee looks pale. Over breakfast, she talks to Dad and Alice about hauntings in a scared voice. They are too rushed to really notice. But this ghost thing is getting out of control.

"Let's go straight to Haunted Guy's after school and work this out," Jessie says in my ear when we're at the bus stop. She's looking at Vee's tired face.

I nod. I want to discover the truth *and* look after Vee. We're on a mission.

Haunted Guy lives on the twelfth floor, at very top of the building (except for the roof). The halls are exactly the same. His door is exactly like ours – without the **dirty fingerprints**.

"What are we gonna say?" whispers Vee, as Jessie holds out her fist to knock on the door.

"We'll tell him the truth," Jessie says, hitching up her rucksack.

"What truth?" I ask, but she's already knocked twice.

Haunted Guy doesn't answer the door. A lady does. She's wearing jeans and a big, bright scarf.

We all smile at her.

"Hello," she says, smiling back. "What can I do for you girls?"

Grown-ups love it when kids make eye contact, **as long as you're smiling.** That's something Mum taught me. Even if you feel shy, look into the grown-up's eyes. Gets 'em every time.

"Um . . . we came to talk to, um . . . the man who lives here about his . . . his . . . missing vase," Jessie says.

The lady chuckles. "You mean you want to know **about the ghost**, right?" she asks. "How did *you* hear about it?"

We all talk at once.

Jessie says, "We live downstairs."

"We saw him in the lobby *right* after it happened," I say.

"The ghost was on our iPad, but we're not allowed to use our iPad anymore," Vee explains.

"All right, all right, **slow down**," the lady says, laughing. "It sounds like we're neighbours. I'm Mina, and the man you saw in the lobby was my brother, Harry. Would you like to come in? Harry is still at work, but you can talk to me."

The apartment is the same shape as ours, but it has about a tenth of the stuff.

"First," Mina says, shoving a laptop aside and putting some crackers on a plate, "the ghost is not real, I promise you. Now sit down."

We all sit around Harry's table.

Vee says, "The ghost *is* real, we saw the security footage."

"You saw the security footage?" Mina looks a bit surprised and glances at the laptop. Then she looks at us with arched eyebrows. "How did you manage that?" Her listening smile reminds me of Mum's when I've come home from some crazy adventure.

Jessie explains about hacking into the security tape and seeing the ghost. Vee tells about Mr Hinkenbushel stopping us and how we're banned from the iPad.

I say, "So Vee thinks it's a ghost, and Jessie thinks it's a hoax to steal the vase. Either way, we know the vase needs to be returned to China. We knew if anyone would care about what we discovered, your brother–"

"Harry," Mina says.

"Harry would care. And–"

"Maybe he'd let us check the security footage again on his computer." Vee nods towards the laptop.

Mina bursts out laughing. "Aren't you girls **sneaky**!" she says. "Listen, I don't have the password for his computer, so we can't check out that security footage. But I promise there's no ghost. OK?"

Vee nods, but I'm annoyed. Even though Mina is funny and nice, we saw the ghost with our own eyes. She doesn't seem to care about the temple at all. She's just making promises with that **grown-up bossiness**, like we should just believe her. Plus, the laptop is **right there**. I bet Jessie could **crack the password**.

Mina is still talking. "There's no way that vase is anything special. I keep telling Harry that Mum bought it from a discount shop, but he has this whole other story in his head."

"Ming Dynasty, acquired during the Opium Wars." Jessie nods, her voice sounding like a teacher's.

Mina looks a bit surprised. People don't expect kids to be as smart as Jessie is. "That's what Harry says, yes."

"But the police must have looked at the security footage too," Jessie insists. "What does Mr Hinkenbushel say?"

"Um . . . the police couldn't really . . . help," Mina says.

Mina looks **surprised** that we know about Mr Hinkenbushel, so I explain.

"He's our next-door neighbour. We hate him so much that we made a **revenge** video about him one time."

Mina laughs again. "You're filmmakers too? I edit video – **documentaries** mostly." She reaches for the laptop but changes her mind, then stands up and opens the door instead. "Well, it's getting late. You should probably be getting home, girls."

She closes the door behind us, and we head down to the lift.

"How can she *know* there's no ghost?" Vee asks, sounding hopeful and nervous at the same time.

"She can't know," I say.

I love the mystery of it. **Haunting or hoax?**

"I bet Mina was looking at the ghost too," Vee says. "Maybe she wants to make a documentary about it."

"If we could just get on the internet," Jessie says. "There has to be something strange about the footage."

The lift isn't coming.

"Stairs?" I suggest, and we turn and take off for the stairwell, rucksacks bouncing on our backs. When we reach the landing, I look up at the last set of stairs before we go down. These stairs are special, because they go to the roof. They're more like a metal ladder, and there's a tall gate in the middle to stop people from going all the way up.

Stuff designed to stop people is cool, because that means it's difficult.

Difficult equals fun. Vee and I look at each other, then toss our rucksacks and race up the metal ladder together. Our shoulders bump and our arms tangle, but Vee beats me to the gate.

"Guys!" Jessie calls from below. "What are you *doing*?"

Vee swings a leg over the gate, then drops down the other side. **Too easy**. I follow, and by the time I'm over, Vee is at the very top landing by the door. We can tell it goes to the outside, because drops of rain are leaking underneath. Also, there's a sign on the door that says in big letters: **Rooftop Access**. It's locked, of course. But that's no problem.

Chapter Eight

"I bet the roof door has the same lock as our balcony," I say, leaping down the stairs two at a time. "And I bet the **hair grip trick** would work for sure."

Vee laughs. "Let's do it!"

Jessie shakes her head at us.

We reach our floor and burst into the hall. Mr Hinkenbushel is at his door, pulling his keys out of his pocket. We stop talking when we see him. He ignores us.

I realize he is the only other person other than Haunted Harry who we *know* has seen the ghost. He was *there*, on the same screen as us.

My heart is all fast and brave from climbing the gate and thinking about the locked door to the roof. I don't stop to think.

"Excuse me, Mr Hinkenbushel."

He turns and glares at me. "What do you want?"

"Um, we were wondering, what are you doing about finding that ghost?"

"Finding what?" He looks at me like I'm an annoying bug.

I don't feel quite so brave anymore, but I keep talking. "The ghost in the security footage. We know you saw it too."

His face gets all red and angry. "I didn't see a ghost, because there was no ghost." He gets **louder** and **redder**, and **spit** starts to gather around the corners of his mouth. "You think you're *so* clever, but you're just nosy, bothersome kids with nothing better to do than–"

"OK, sorry!" I say.

We dash through our own door while he's still shouting.

"Subtle move, Squishy Taylor," Jessie says, and we all laugh.

When I Skype Mum in the living room, everyone wants to talk to her. Alice comes over with a basket of laundry and starts asking about the economy. Mum loves to talk about the economy. Alice stays until every sock is folded. I even help, so she'll go away faster. Mum doesn't notice.

When Alice finally leaves, Jessie brings Baby over. He **bangs on** the iPad. Mum laughs at how cute he is.

Then she has to go to a meeting. "Love you, Squishy-sweet," she says, blowing me a kiss.

When she hangs up, it makes me want to cry.

It feels like Geneva is on Pluto, rather than just a plane ride away.

I'm still annoyed about missing out on **Mum-time** when it's time to go to bed. I curl up into a little ball on my blanket. No one notices. But I notice when Vee takes the torch up to her bunk.

I ask, "What's that for?"

"Nothing," she mutters. "Just so I can see stuff if I need to see."

Dad starts to do his round of bedtime **forehead-kisses**, but I duck my face away at the last minute.

"**What's up, Squisho?**"

"Nothing," I mutter, just the way Vee muttered to me. I want him to reach in and give me a real Dad-cuddle. But he just leaves.

I can't sleep because I'm annoyed about sharing my mum and dad. I'm annoyed about Mum laughing with Jessie about Baby. I squeeze my eyes closed. I try to think about the vase mystery instead, but it's not fun. **It's just scary**. I roll over and pull my blankets tighter.

I wake up to a **light darting** around the room. It takes me a moment to realize it's Vee with the torch. What's she doing? She flicks it off after a minute, and I lie in the dark.

The bunk bed ladder starts creaking, and our bedroom door slowly opens and closes. **Vee is sneaking out.**

I'm thinking about following her, but before I can, she comes back in. Dad, stumbling and sleepy, is with her. He stands by our bed, saying, "It's four in the morning, sweetie. There are no ghosts. Just go back to sleep."

He's using his special Dad-voice. The Dad-voice he only uses for **ME**. It makes me remember all of the things I was angry about before I fell asleep.

After he leaves, I can't hold the hot anger in anymore.

"He's not your dad, you know," I say.

"Wha-what?" Vee asks.

"You think you can have my dad? Well, you can't. He's mine."

Jessie rolls over in the bunk below mine. "What are you guys talking about?" she asks sleepily.

Vee says, "I just had a bad dream."

She sounds like a whiny little kid. Which is annoying.

"All I'm saying is that he's my dad, not yours," I say.

"Squishy!" Jessie says. "Don't be so selfish. Vee's just scared-"

"Me? Selfish? You're the selfish one! You stole all my Mum-time tonight and didn't even *think* about what you were doing."

"**Whoa!**" Jessie says. "Squishy, it's the middle of the night, and you're being really weird."

I don't say anything.

But then I say, "I'm not talking to you guys." Just in case they don't understand the silence.

I realize Vee is crying. Sometimes I'm so much more mature than she is.

"Vee?" Jessie says. "What's up?"

Vee takes a **little sob-breath**. "It's the ghost. I can't sleep because of it."

"There is no ghost," Jessie says.

"But we **saw** it," Vee insists.

"We saw a *video*," Jessie says. "It could have been anything."

Vee keeps crying. Even though it's annoying, I start to feel sorry for her. I'm angry and twitchy and itchy. I need to do something.

"Maybe we *should* try to scare off the ghost," I say, because there's something scary—exciting about the idea.

Jessie is silent.

"Jessie?" Vee asks.

"OK, fine," Jessie says. "There's no ghost. But we can do it if you really want."

"Can we do it now?" Vee asks. "I can't sleep anymore."

"Yes," Jessie says. "Where?"

I know exactly where.

"We have to be absolutely alone," I say. "We have to go up on the roof."

Chapter Nine

We tiptoe around the dark kitchen with the torch, looking for good things to take. Jessie finds a hair grip, and Vee gets our old brown recipe book with the gold writing on the front.

"This one's just like the big book in the film," she whispers.

I pull open the spice drawer. There was turmeric and holy basil at my grandmother's funeral. I know funerals are different from **ghost ceremonies**, but they're both for saying goodbye to dead people. I want to take candles and the lighter with us, even though we're not allowed to use them. Jessie makes me put them back in the drawer where I got them. **She's so bossy**.

Jessie slides everything into a green bag, and then she spots the iPad. She grabs it, and I take the key off the hook by the door.

We tiptoe out into the dimly lit hall and down to the bright stairwell. We run up to the ladder.

I climb the gate easily, and Vee follows me. Jessie reaches up to pass the bag to me. She starts climbing but stops with one leg over the top.

"I'm stuck," she says. She's holding on tight, and she doesn't want to lift her other leg over the gate.

"Come on," Vee says. "Just hold tight and lift your foot."

Jessie's knuckles are white. She's almost lying along the top of the gate, and the foot near me keeps trying to find a new spot. She looks like she doesn't trust herself to put it down.

I remember how scared I was looking down from our balcony, how **shaky** and **slippery** my hands felt.

"You're OK," I say. I move so I'm under her. "Step on me."

I guide her foot and hold it steady on my shoulder.

"Uhhhh . . ." she says. "Is that OK?"

She's kind of heavy, and her foot is **smashing** my ear.

"It's fine," I say. "Just a bit squishy."

Jessie does a half-laugh, half-grunt, and then she's over the top and climbing down the other side. Her foot **catches my curls** and yanks at them.

"Ow!"

"Sorry!"

The three of us stand there, breathless, by the **Rooftop Access** sign.

"You better be able to pick that lock," Jessie says.

Just like I thought, the lock is the same as the one on our balcony. All it takes is just the right **twist and jiggle** of the hair grip, and I'm done. Awesome. I push the door, and it swings open.

We're out on the roof. It's wide with a wall all around the edge. The main thing I notice is the city, spreading out beyond the wall. It's huge and sparkling with lights as far as I can see.

"Eeee!" squeals Vee, running out across the clear space and spinning around in circles.

It has stopped raining, and the air is cold and clear. I can hear cars below us, but the sound is so far away.

Behind us, the door we came out of looks like the entry to a little shed.

It's the perfect place.

Vee **scatters a circle** with the basil and places the recipe book perfectly in the middle. I mark our foreheads with turmeric, **swiping up** with my finger like they did at my grandma's funeral.

Jessie hunches over the iPad.

"What are you doing?" I ask, leaning over her shoulder.

"Getting the footage of the ghost," she says. "Hang on. It's pretty low on battery, but . . . here we go."

The ghost is still there, standing tall and still on the screen. We all stare at it as it fades to white and disappears into an empty hall.

Then Jessie touches the screen. "I'll put it on repeat," she says. We watch, **mesmerized**, as the ghost appears and disappears. Jessie places the iPad beside the recipe book in the middle of the circle.

"Hands on the book," Vee says as we sit cross-legged around it. We place our fingers on the cover. Vee looks up and says, "Now we need to chant."

"Chant what?" Jessie asks, looking a bit embarrassed.

My grandmother chanted the sacred "*Om Namah Shivaya*" when she prayed, but that doesn't seem right.

"Could we just say, 'go away ghost'?" Vee asks.

But I shake my head. "We don't just want it to go away," I say. "We want justice. We want to be able to return the vase to the temple."

Then Jessie gets inspired. She's good with words. "OK. We want it gone. We want justice. 'Ghost be gone and justice will follow.' How's that?"

Vee grins, and I say, "Perfect."

So we all chant together:

"Ghost be gone
and justice will follow.
Ghost be gone
and justice will follow.
Ghost be gone
and justice will follow."

We sway around the recipe book with the screen light shining up on our faces. Jessie is looking down at the iPad, and Vee and I are looking out into the darkness. My voice sounds different and special when it's exactly in time with the others. The **night feels enormous** around us. Our voices get louder and louder until it feels like something big will happen. The wind blows through our hair, smelling of dried basil. We slowly stop chanting.

Everything feels quiet and good.

"Do you think it worked?" Vee asks.

I nod. I think it must have.

Jessie is still focused on the iPad. "Hey," she says, snatching it up. "It **was a hoax!** Look – the video has been edited."

She points her finger at the doorframe behind the ghost. The frame jumps sideways when the ghost appears, and the shadows get darker in a flash. It jumps back again when the ghost disappears.

"Someone pasted video over the top here," Jessie says. We stare as it loops again, and the doorframe jumps.

"There was no ghost?" Vee asks.

"No ghost," I say. I'm actually kind of disappointed.

"But there was *someone* who edited the video and stole a vase," Jessie says, as if to make me feel better.

The iPad's battery is showing just a two-per cent charge. I watch the video repeat over and over again. There's not enough battery and still a mystery to solve.

Then, out of nowhere: **BANG!**

The Rooftop Access door at the top of the stairs slams shut.

Vee screams. We all scramble to our feet and run for the little shed.

There's no handle on the outside of the door. Nothing to pull on. Just a keyhole. We grope down the sides, trying to squeeze our fingers in the tiny gaps.

It's no use.

We're stuck here on the roof.

Chapter Ten

"Help! HELP!" Vee shouts as we all run to the edge of the building. The wall is concrete and comes up to my chest. I have to stand on tiptoe to see the street at all. The few tiny people under the streetlamps don't look up. Anyway, if they did look up, they wouldn't see us up here in the dark.

"Do you think the ghost locked us up here?" Vee asks.

"No!" Jessie says. "There is no ghost, remember? Someone edited the video."

For the first time, I feel a little bit scared. I glance at the closed door. "Do you think the person who made the video locked us up here?" I ask.

"No!" Jessie says. "It was the wind. It was our fault for not propping it open."

I think she's probably right. But we're **stuck on a roof** in the dark. So it's a bit scary anyway.

Suddenly, all I want is my Mum. And the iPad is right here. I grab it.

"Yes!" Jessie says. "Message Mum."

But I'm not messaging their mum, Alice. I tap through to Skype.

Bloobleep bloobleep.

"Squishy, no," Jessie says.

But it's already connecting.

Mum's face comes up. She's not at her desk. She's at home with wet hair and in her dressing gown.

For one second she squints at me, looking confused.

Then the iPad goes black with a little white spinning circle in the centre. It's run out of battery.

"Why did you do that, Squishy?" Jessie says. "Skype uses up so much power."

We watch the last light on the screen fade. This is it. Now we're really alone up here. The black screen reminds me of not getting to talk with Mum. It reminds me of not getting special Dad-cuddles. I bite my lip. My eyes get blurry with tears. My parents have deserted me.

Jessie is frowning. "We need to get a message to someone."

She tries to turn on the iPad again, but the battery is definitely dead. Vee rips pages out of the recipe book. She runs to the edge and starts folding a paper aeroplane. She aims it down to try and get someone's attention, but it just death-spirals into the darkness.

I watch it go and think it needs a message. I try to write HELP on the next one with wet turmeric instead of a pen, but it ends up a big yellow mess. Jessie stands beside me, flashing the torch towards the street, but nobody notices.

Finally we slide down with our backs against the wall. I'm out of ideas. This has stopped being a fun adventure.

It feels like we're going to be here for the **rest of our lives**. I'm getting cold. I don't even care about the missing vase anymore. I just want to go home and eat breakfast.

Vee shivers. She says, "I'm hungry."

I realize I can see her face. "It's starting to get light," I say. The sky is turning pale pink all across the horizon.

"We have to figure out some sort of way to get **out of here**," Jessie says. "Mum and Tom will wake up soon."

I stand up and lean my elbows on the wall, looking across the street. The angles of the buildings and the trees below look very familiar.

"Is that Not-Boring Lady's office?" Vee asks, joining me and pointing.

She's right, it is. And Not-Boring Lady is already at work. She must start early. She's directly across from us, and two floors below. Which means...

"That must be **Haunted Harry's** balcony right down there," Jessie says.

We are looking straight down at a balcony with a table and some plants.

And in the middle of the balcony is a big white vase with blue decorations.

Chapter Eleven

Vee stares down at the vase. "We brought it back. We did it."

"Vee!" Jessie's got her grown-up voice back. **"There was no ghost."**

"Anyway," I say, "we haven't finished the job yet. The vase needs to go back to the temple in China."

We all lean out, looking down at the vase glowing white in the orange sunrise. Along the wall are the remnants of us trying to signal our way out: the torn recipe book, the torch, the turmeric.

"We **can't do anything** while we're stuck here," Jessie says. She starts waving the torch towards Not-Boring Lady. But it's not going to work. Not-Boring Lady never answers our signals.

"We're going to have to climb down to Haunted Harry's balcony," Vee says.

Jessie is horrified. **"That's insane!"**

It's actually not. From Haunted Harry's balcony to here is nowhere near as high as the rock climbing walls we practise on. I can see some good handholds in the stone. If you fell, **you'd only fall** as far as the balcony.

"It'll be easy," Vee says, jutting her chin out. "I'm going to save us."

"Vee, please don't be crazy," Jessie says, pulling her arm back.

Squishy Taylor to the rescue. I put my palms on top of the wall and jump up, pushing down until my arms are straight. My tummy is bent over the wall. I lift one leg to swing it over.

Jessie shouts, "No, Squishy, stop it!" and grabs my leg.

That's the moment I knock over the jar of turmeric.

It drops down the side of the building, bounces off Haunted Harry's balcony rail and keeps falling. The lid flies off the jar, and the powder glides out in a huge, spiralling, yellow cloud. The cloud gets bigger and bigger as it floats silently towards the ground.

And now, finally, Not-Boring Lady has noticed us. She stands at her window, staring first at the cloud and then up at us. I wave wildly, **clinging to the wall** with my knees. Not-Boring Lady runs for her phone. She's waving back at us with crazy, flinging hands, as if she could push us away from the edge of the wall.

"**Hey!**" It's Haunted Harry. "What are you kids doing?" He's in his pyjamas on his balcony, staring up at us. He must have heard the jar of turmeric hit the railing.

"We're stuck!" Vee yells.

"We can't get down!" I shout.

"Well, for crying out loud, you girls! **Do NOT try to climb down** to the balcony!" he yells back up at us.

Mina appears beside him. She stares up at us before running back inside.

"Wait right there!" Haunted Harry yells.

So we wait.

The first person to run out of the Rooftop Access door is Dad. He runs right past my bonus sisters and pulls me up into **the biggest hug ever.**

"We woke up, and you were gone," he says with his mouth in my hair. "I was so worried." He squeezes me really tight.

Now I know **I'll always be special** to my dad, no matter how many bonus sisters I have.

Alice is **cuddling** Jessie and Vee.

Haunted Harry, Mina and Not-Boring Lady are right behind her. We all stand on the roof, laughing and talking. Dad doesn't let me go for a long, long time. Even when he stops hugging me, he keeps holding my hand.

"How did you find us?" I ask. "Did Not-Boring Lady or Haunted Harry call?"

"They both got us pretty quickly," Dad says. "But do you know who called first?"

I look at him, not sure.

"Your mum," he says.

I smile. Now I really, truly don't feel deserted anymore.

"The vase," I say remembering why we're here. "It came back!"

I try to drag Dad over to the edge to look, but he doesn't move.

Alice holds up a hand. "Wait a second, Squishy Taylor. **First things first**. What on Earth are you three doing up here?"

We don't even know where to start. Vee garbles out the story of our ceremony to get rid of the ghost. Jessie makes sure everyone knows she never believed in the ghost. I interrupt to explain to Mina about being banned from talking to my mum (which Alice tries to explain isn't exactly true). We all tell Not-Boring Lady how many times we tried to signal her. She's the only one in daytime clothes, but it's like **one big pyjama party** up here on the rooftop. The grown-ups are rolling with laughter one minute and **intrigued** the next.

"But we still don't know who edited the security footage," Alice says.

"*That's* what I want to know," Jessie says. "It had to be someone with access to the footage who wanted the vase."

I'm struck by something. "We know somebody who had access to the footage, and **really didn't want us** to look at the video," I say.

They all smile and wait for me to answer. "Mr Hinkenbushel!" I say.

"Squishy!" Jessie laughs. "We know Mr Hinkenbushel isn't the bad guy."

Mina coughs, looking embarrassed. **"It was me,"** she says. "I secretly took the vase to be valued. I *knew* Harry was wrong. In the meantime, I thought I'd play a trick on him–"

Harry grins. "I loved it!" he says. "And so, clearly, did these girls."

"We explained it to the police on the first day," Mina says. "I had no idea there was a whole ghost adventure going on until yesterday," she says to the grown-ups. Then she grins at us. "But now I know that, I'll never try to keep a secret from you girls again."

I can't tell if I'm disappointed that there is no ghost or happy to be friends with a hacker and documentary maker. Jessie has already got a billion questions for Mina on the tip of her tongue. But she'll have to wait. There are more important things than computer tricks right now.

"And now," I say, turning towards Not-Boring Lady, because I'm sure she will help us, "we have to return the vase to China."

But Mina gets our attention with a shake of her head and a laugh that sounds half disappointed. "I'm sorry to say that the vase was a fake. Mum really did buy it from a discount shop!" she says.

Everybody laughs. Our big adventure on the roof feels **scary** and **exciting** enough that I don't even mind.

Not-Boring Lady clears her throat. When she has our attention, she pulls a **huge red scarf** out of her briefcase and hands it to Jessie. "From now on," she says, "any time you girls want to contact me, hang this scarf in your window. I promise to look up from my typing once every hour."

Jessie, Vee and I thank her. Alice tells her she doesn't need to do that.

Mina turns to Dad. "I can show you how to lock your iPad so it only accesses Skype," she says to him while winking at me. "Then Squishy Taylor can call her Mum in private without getting into other kinds of trouble."

I suddenly realize something is missing. "Where's Baby?" I ask.

Dad and Alice look at each other.

"He was asleep," Alice says at the same time Dad says, "We forgot him."

We all run for the stairs, with Alice and Dad leading the crowd.

The door to our apartment is wide open. We all look in and stare. Standing in the middle of the kitchen in his pyjamas,

holding a **giggling** and **gurgling** Baby, is
Mr Hinkenbushel.

About the author and illustrator

Ailsa Wild is an acrobat, whip cracker and teaching artist who ran away from the circus to become a writer. She taught Squishy all her best bunk-bed tricks.

Ben Wood started drawing when he was Baby's age and happily drew all over his mum and dad's walls! Since then, he has never stopped drawing. He has an identical twin, and they used to play all kinds of pranks on their younger brother.

Author acknowledgements

Christy and Luke, for writing residencies, bunk-bed acrobatics and the day you turned the truck around.

Antoni, Penni, Moreno and the masterclass crew, for showing me what the journey could be. Here's to epiphanies.

Indira and Devika, because she couldn't be real without you.

Hilary, Marisa, Penny, Sarah and the HGE team, for making it happen. What an amazing net to have landed in.

Ben, for bringing them all to life.

Jono, for independence and supporting each other's dreams.

— Ailsa

Illustrator acknowledgements

Hilary, Marisa, Sarah and the HGE team, for your enthusiasm and spark.

Penny, for being the best! Thanks for inviting me along on this Squish-tastic ride! (And for putting up with all my emails!)

Ailsa, for creating such a fun place for me to play in.

John, for listening to me ramble on and on about Squishy Taylor every day.

– Ben

Talk about it!

1. Squishy Taylor and her bonus sisters love adventure. What is the adventure in this story? In what ways did the girls put themselves in danger because of the adventure?

2. This story is about a ghost and an adventure. But the girls also learned some interesting history. What did they learn?

3. The ceremony the girls hold to get rid of the ghost doesn't quite go as they plan. Talk about what they used in the ceremony, what helped and what didn't.

Write about it!

1. The girls lose their iPad privileges. Why? Write about a time you lost a privilege and how you got it back.

2. In this story, the vase turns out to be a fake. But what if it had been real? Write a different ending.

3. Squishy feels like her parents have deserted her. What happens that leads her to believe this? Think about a time when you felt bad. How did you make the situation better?